Ready for reading

Jenny Tyler and Robyn Gee

Designed and illustrated by Graham Round

With consultant advice from Gillian Hartley and John Newson
of the Child Development Research Unit at Nottingham University

About this book

This book is for an adult and child to use together. It is
designed to help young children practise some of the skills
which build towards reading and to give them the confidence
to read their first words.

Notes for parents

Learning to read is a gradual process which involves bringing together a lot of different skills. The activities in this book help give practice with some of these.

Pre-reading skills

In the first part of the book there are several activities to help your child develop the basic reasoning skills and visual awareness of shape and detail that she needs before she can start recognizing letter and word shapes.

There are also picture sequencing activities. These help children to learn to "read" pictures to find out what is happening in a story, and are useful for giving them the confidence to attempt to read the words that go with pictures.

Putting pictures in the right order helps to reinforce the left to right movement in reading and the idea that things only make sense if they are in the right order.

Word and letter matching

The second part of the book moves on to a range of word and letter matching activities.

Finding pairs of matching words and letters is a shape-matching activity which helps children to familiarize themselves with word and letter shapes.

Matching an initial letter to an object is a useful ability which helps children to learn the sound made by each letter. This is more important at first than knowing letter names, though children do not usually find it difficult to learn letter sounds and letter names almost at the same time.

Using this book

Make sure that using this book is an enjoyable experience for both you and your child. Take your time over each page and don't try to do too much at once.

Talk about the pictures together before trying to answer any of the questions. For example, on pages 10 and 11 talk about what is happening in each picture, before trying to put the pictures in the right order.

Your child may sometimes come up with answers that, while unexpected, are perfectly plausible. Don't tell her she is wrong, but you could point out that there is another possible answer.

If your child seems unready or unwilling to tackle any of the activities, leave them and come back to them another day.

Small letters

Small (lower case) letters have been used throughout this book as it is best to concentrate on these to start with. They give words distinctive shapes, whereas capitals make words uniform in shape.

Following up

There are many ways in which you can follow up the activities in this book. Draw your child's attention, for instance, to the way in which written words are used in all sorts of everyday situations, such as shopping and cooking, signs and advertisements.

Writing things down for children is a good way of getting them interested in words.

Write captions for pictures your child has drawn. Get her to tell you exactly what to say.

The best thing you can do though is to read and enjoy books with your child. A child who has learnt that books can be a source of pleasure will have a strong incentive to learn to read.

Spot the difference

● There are five differences between these two pictures. Can you find them all? Ring them on the bottom picture.

Find the missing pieces

- Find the pieces that belong to the big picture.
  Colour them in.

4

● Find the pieces that belong to the big picture.
Colour them in.

Picture sequences

• What are cat and mouse doing in these pictures?

The present

1

2

3

The window cleaner

1

2

3

• Tell the stories.

● What are cat and mouse doing in these pictures?

Mouse rides his bike

1

2

3

The kite

1

2

3

● Tell the stories.

Odd picture out

● Find the odd one out in each row and colour it.

● Find the odd one out in each row and colour it.

Mixed up pictures

● These pictures are in the wrong order. Talk about each picture. Work out the right order. Write numbers 1, 2 and 3 in the boxes.

Cat's cake

2   1   3

Mouse and the flowers

3   1   2

Find the letters

- Choose a letter from the bottom of the page to match each row. Colour its card to match the rest of the cards in the row.

12

Odd letter out

- Can you find the odd letter out in each row?
  Colour it in.

Whose balloon?

dog snail rabbit pig mouse cat

spider

mouse dog rabbit cat

spider pig snail

- Join the balloons to their owners by drawing the strings.

- One animal doesn't have a balloon. Who is it?
  Draw one for him.

- Colour the balloons.

14

Whose luggage?

Cat and mouse are going on holiday with their friends.

- Draw a line to join each animal to his luggage.

Letter game

See if you can help cat and mouse with this game.

- Look at the word under each picture. Now find a letter card to match each letter in the word, and make it the same colour.

- There is one letter too many. Colour it pink.

t b a r e

tree   boat   car

c e o t a r

fish   house   bee

Shopping lists

Cat and mouse have been shopping.

shopping list
- juice ✓
- milk ✓
- flour ✓
- beans ✓
- crisps ✓
- cat food ✓
- chocolate ✓
- coffee ✓

- Did cat buy everything on his shopping list?
  Tick each item on the list and in the box next to it, as you find it.

18

- Did mouse buy everything on his shopping list?
- What did he buy that was not on his list? Write it on the list.

Match letters and pictures

- Each letter has a picture of something which begins with it.
  Draw a line from each letter to its picture.

The birthday party

Cat, mouse, frog and pig are having a birthday party.

- Look at the name cards and work out where each of them should sit. Draw a line from each animal to his chair.

- Can you work out which hat belongs to each animal? Colour cat's hat yellow. Colour pig's hat blue.

- Whose birthday is it? How old is he?

happy
birthday
cat

love
from

m o u s e

happy
birthday

love
from

p i g

happy
birthday
cat

love
from

f r o g

● Frog, pig and mouse haven't finished writing their
birthday cards. Can you help them?

Going home

Mouse, pig and frog are going home.
There is a balloon and party bag for each of them –
and for cat too.

- Draw a string from each animal to his balloon.

- Colour each animal's party bag to match his coat.

- Colour cat's party bag pink.